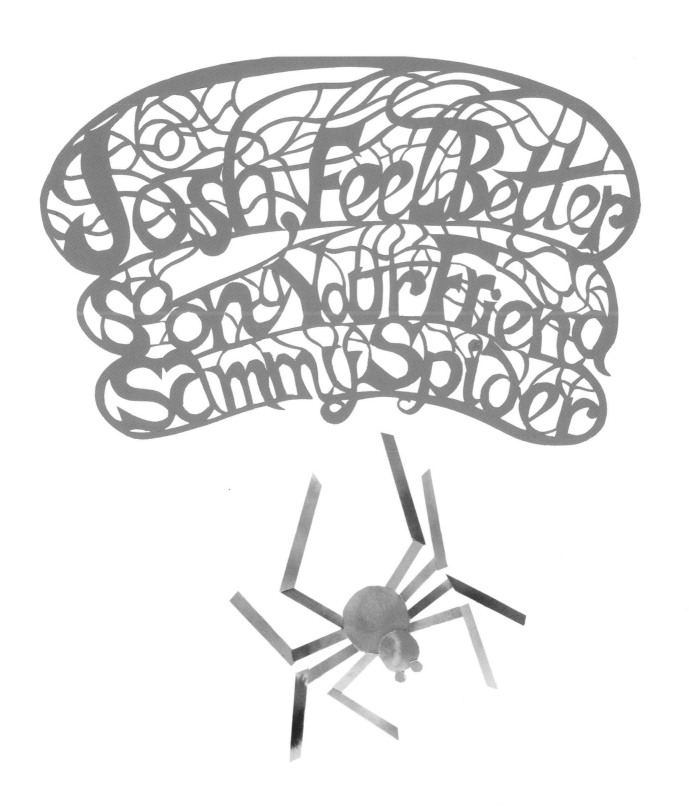

To Hayden, Derek, and Leo who love performing mitzvot and
bringing joy to others.

—S.A.R.

To Judye Groner and Madeline Wickler who brought Jewish
children's publishing out of the Middle Ages and me into it.

—K.J.K.

KAR-BEN PUBLISHING
A division of Lerner Publishing Group, Inc.
241 First Avenue North
Minneapolis, MN 55401 U.S.A.
1-800-4-KARBEN

Website address: www.karben.com

Library of Congress Cataloging-in-Publication Data

Rouss, Sylvia A.
   Sammy Spider's first Mitzvah / by Sylvia A. Rouss ; illustrated
by Katherine Janus Kahn.
      pages   cm
   Summary: "Sammy Spider visits a sick friend and learns about
doing good deeds.
   ISBN 978–1–4677–1947–6 (lib. bdg. : alk. paper)
   ISBN 978–1–4677–4672–4 (eBook)
   [1. Spiders—Fiction. 2. Sick—Fiction. 3. Judaism—Customs
and practices—Fiction. 4. Jews—United States—Fiction.
5. Conduct of life—Fiction.] I. Kahn, Katherine, illustrator.
II. Title.
PZ7.R7622Sae 2014
[E]—dc23   2013021755

Manufactured in the United States of America
1 – VI – 7/15/14

SAMMY SPIDER'S

FIRST

MITZVAH

Sylvia A. Rouss

Illustrated by
Katherine Janus Kahn

KAR-BEN
PUBLISHING

UP A SICK FRIEND

Sammy Spider heard a loud
"ACHOO!" He looked down from
his web and saw Josh Shapiro
curled up on the couch below.

Again Sammy heard the sound. "ACHOO!"

"Mother!" shouted Sammy. "What's wrong with Josh?

"He caught a cold," answered Mrs. Spider.

"Can I catch a cold, too?" asked Sammy.

Mrs. Spider laughed. "Silly little Sammy. Spider's don't catch colds. Spiders catch flies. And for that, we need to spin a web."

Mrs. Shapiro walked into the room. "Time for your medicine, Josh," she said, feeling his head. "I think you may still have a fever. This will make you feel better."

Sammy gave Mrs. Spider a puzzled look. "Josh is sick," explained Mrs. Spider. "And the medicine helps him."

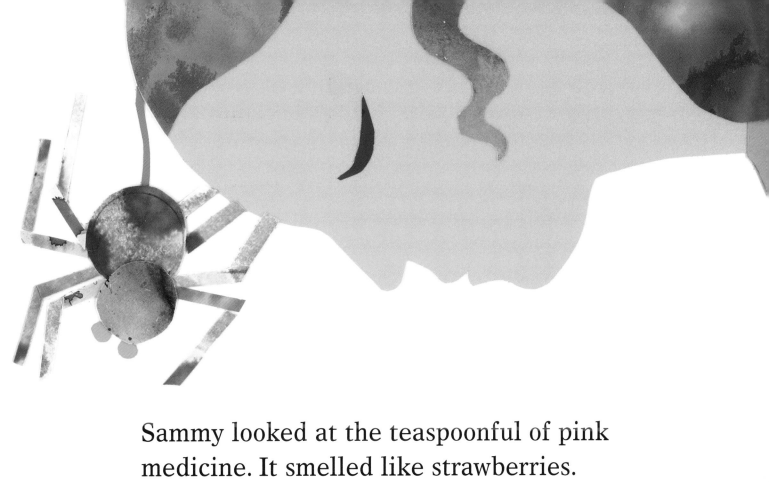

Sammy looked at the teaspoonful of pink medicine. It smelled like strawberries.
"Can I have some medicine, too?" he asked.

"Silly little Sammy. Spiders don't take medicine. Spiders spin webs!"

Just then the doorbell rang. Mrs. Shapiro opened the door. It was their new neighbor from Israel. "Hi, Moti!" she exclaimed.

Sammy was excited. "Look, Mother. Moti is here, but Josh can't play. He's sick."

"When someone is sick, it is a mitzvah to visit them," Mrs. Spider replied.

Sammy saw Moti give Mrs. Shapiro a covered dish. "My mommy asked me to bring this chicken soup for Josh. Chicken soup always makes me feel better when I have a cold," said Moti.

Josh waved at Moti from the couch. "Thank you for the soup. Chicken soup is my favorite! But don't come any closer. I don't want you to catch my cold. ACHOO!"

"LABRIUT," said Moti. "It means 'to your health.' It's the Hebrew word you say when someone sneezes. "I hope you feel better soon," Moti said, waving good-bye.

Mrs. Shapiro put the chicken soup in a bowl for Josh. "It's yummy!" said Josh, slurping a spoonful.

Sammy smelled the delicious soup. "Mother, may I have some chicken soup, too?" he asked.

"Silly little Sammy. Spiders don't eat soup. Spiders eat flies. And for that we need to spin a web."

"How can I help Josh feel better?" Sammy asked. "How can I do a mitzvah?"

"Why don't you spin a web for him?" suggested Mrs. Spider.

Sammy waited for Josh to finish his soup, and then he hovered above Josh's head and began spinning. Josh giggled as the little spider happily spun a web.

Sammy was so busy spinning that he didn't hear Mr. Shapiro come home. Mr. Shapiro smiled at Josh. "You look like you're feeling a little better," he said, handing him a gift.

Mrs. Spider slid down to hug Sammy.
"I think your spinning really helped Josh."

Sammy watched Josh
unwrap a toy train.

"Mother, what is that?"
asked Sammy.

A CHOO-CHOO Labriut!

"A CHOO-CHOO!"
she answered.

"LABRIUT, Mother!"
Sammy shouted.
"To your health!"

Bikkur cholim is the mitzvah of visiting the sick to bring them comfort and make them feel better. It is a moral and spiritual obligation for all Jews. The Bible instructs us to aspire to be like God, who visited Abraham while he was sick (Genesis 17:26-18:1). By fulfilling this role, we deeply enrich both our lives and the lives of those we visit. Bikkur cholim is an easy mitzvah for children to perform. They can visit sick friends and family, comfort them by phone, send cards or e-mails, or offer to bring home their homework or to help with pets while they're sick.

About the Author

Sylvia A. Rouss is the award-winning author of many children's books, including the popular *Sammy Spider* series. *The Littlest Pair* won the National Jewish Book Award and *Sammy Spider's First Trip to Israel* was named a Sydney Taylor Honor book by the Association of Jewish Libraries. Sylvia lives in Los Angeles.

About the Illustrator

Katherine Janus Kahn has illustrated more than 30 picture books, toddler board books, holiday services, and activity books. She and Sammy Spider frequently visit schools and bookstores for storytelling and "chalk talks." Katherine also paints and sculpts. She lives in Wheaton, Maryland.